Presented to

_____

by_____

on_____

I'm Parker!

I LIKE TO THINK ABOUT IT

Crystal Bowman
Illustrated by Elena Kucharik

Tyndale House Publishers, Inc.
WHEATON, ILLINOIS

Visit Tyndale's exciting Web site at www.tyndale.com

Edited by Betty Free Swanberg
Designed by Catherine Bergstrom

Library of Congress Cataloging-in-Publication Data
Bowman, Crystal.
    I'm Parker!: I like to think about it / Crystal Bowman ; illustrated by Elena Kucharik.
        p. cm. — (Little blessings)
Summary: In rhyming text, Parker describes some of his wonder about God's world and
how excited he is to learn more about it.
    ISBN 0-8423-7674-7 (alk. paper)
    1. Wonder in children—Religious aspects—Christianity—Juvenile literature. [1. Wonder.
2. Curiosity. 3. Christian life.] I. Kucharik, Elena, ill. II. Title. III. Series: Little blessings
picture books.

    BF723.W65B69 2003
    242'.62—dc21   2002015177

Printed in Italy

09 08 07 06 05 04 03
7 6 5 4 3 2 1

To Betty and Karen for helping me to think about it.

Lead me by your truth and teach me.

PSALM 25.5

I am Parker.
   How are you?
Why are all
   your feathers blue?
I can climb,
   but you can fly—
It makes me think
   and wonder why.

How do apples
  grow on trees?
May I pick some,
  pretty please?
Are they ready?
  There's no doubt—
These are things
  I think about.

Icy, frosty
    winter fun,
Throwing snowballs
    one by one.
Why does God make
    winter weather?
How do snowballs
    stick together?

7

Excuse me,
    can you tell me how
My milk comes from
    a big, brown cow

Or cows with spots
    of black and white?
I wonder where
    cows sleep at night.

9

Watching pebbles
  skip and hop,
I wonder how
  they stay on top.
But down they *plop*—
  and then I think,
Why do pebbles
  finally sink?

Hey, let's play
    a guessing game!
Do you think
    God knows my name?
Zoë's telling
    Jack a secret.
Do you think
    that he can keep it?

13

In the garden,
    planting seeds,
Scooping dirt,
    and pulling weeds—
Lord, I'd really
    like to know
How you make
    the flowers grow.

14

15

"Let's have fun!"
    I say to Jack.
Sneak a worm
    down Kaitlyn's back!
Will she run
    or will she shout?
These are things
    I think about.

18

Time for lunch
    and something sweet.
Where does food go
    when we eat?
What is cold
    and what is hot?
What tastes good
    and what does not?

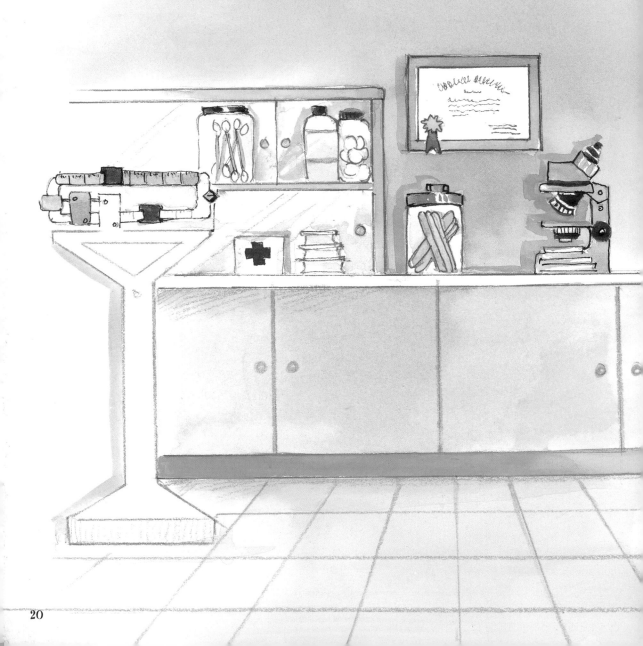

Take a picture—
    look and see.
I wonder what's
    inside of me.
My heart is beating;
    see my spine?
Everything is
    working fine.

See me bouncing
    on my bed?
How does Jack
    stand on his head?
What is high
    and what is low?
These are things
    I'd like to know.

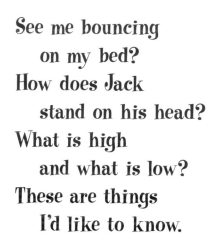

I think my shoes
    are getting tight!
Am I growing
    overnight?

I'll have to find
another pair.
Does anyone
have shoes to share?

Lord, I know
    that I can pray
For all the children
    far away.

Do they play,
   and do they run?
Are they like me—
   do they have fun?

Fish have fins
    instead of feet.
I wonder what
    they like to eat.
Why do fish
    have shiny scales?
See them swish
    their swishy tails?

How does all
　　the land and sea
End up where
　　it ought to be?
Where do waves go
　　as they roar,
Splashing on
　　the sandy shore?

I like to think
  about the day
When I'll work
  instead of play—
"Dr. Parker's
  coming through!
I will take
  good care of you."

35

Stars are shining
   in the sky.
Can I count them?
   I can try!
Twenty-eight and
   ninety-four,
Fifty billion—
   maybe more!

How many lambs
    are in a row,
All tucked in
    from head to toe?
S-h-h-h, it's time
    to take a rest.
Cozy blankets
    are the best!

Dear God, you made
    the earth and skies,
And you're the one
    who makes me wise.
Teach me, as
    I live and grow,
All the things
    that I should know.

About the Author

Crystal Bowman received a bachelor of arts degree in elementary education from Calvin College and studied early childhood development at the University of Michigan. A former preschool teacher, she loves writing for young children and is the author of numerous children's books. Crystal is a writer and speaker for MOPS International and has written several books in the recently published MOPS picture-book series.

Besides writing books, Crystal enjoys being active in the local schools, speaking at authors' assemblies, and conducting poetry workshops. Her books of humorous poetry are favorites in the classroom as well as at literacy conferences.

Crystal is also involved in women's ministries, writing Bible study materials for her church and speaking at women's conferences. She has been a guest on many Christian radio programs and has written a book of meditations for moms.

Crystal and her husband live in Grand Rapids, Michigan, and have three grown children.

About the Illustrator

Elena Kucharik, well-known Care Bears artist, has created the Little Blessings characters, which appear in a line of Little Blessings products for young children and their families.

Born in Cleveland, Ohio, Elena received a bachelor of fine arts degree in commercial art at Kent State University. After graduation she worked as a greeting card artist and art director at American Greetings Corporation in Cleveland.

For the past 25 years Elena has been a freelance illustrator. During this time she was the lead artist and developer of Care Bears, as well as a designer and illustrator for major corporations and publishers. For the last 10 years Elena has been focusing her talents on illustrations for children's books.

Elena and her husband live in Madison, Connecticut, and have two grown daughters.

Products in the Little Blessings line

Bible for Little Hearts
Prayers for Little Hearts
Promises for Little Hearts
Lullabies for Little Hearts
Lullabies Cassette

Blessings Everywhere
Rain or Shine
God Makes Nighttime Too
Birthday Blessings
Christmas Blessings
God Loves You
Thank You, God!
ABC's
Count Your Blessings
Blessings Come in Shapes
Many-Colored Blessings

What Is God Like?
Who Is Jesus?
What about Heaven?
Are Angels Real?
What Is Prayer?

I'm Kaitlyn!
I'm Zoë!
I'm Jack!
I'm Parker!

Little Blessings New Testament
    & Psalms

Blessings Every Day
Questions from Little Hearts

God Created Me!
    A memory book of baby's first year